It was the day before Easter in April Valley. Colonel Wellington B. Bunny was deciding who should replace him as Chief Easter Bunny.

It was a very difficult decision because it was a very important job. The Chief Easter Bunny was in charge of carving chocolates, sewing bonnets—and, of course, decorating and delivering Easter eggs.

After much careful thought, the Colonel made his decision. He chose a young bunny named Peter Cottontail.

Meanwhile, a terrible, wicked, nasty rabbit named Irontail had other ideas. "According to the constitution of April Valley," Irontail announced, "the Chief Easter Bunny shall be the one who delivers the most eggs."

Irontail challenged Peter to an egg-delivering contest that would take place the very next day.
"I'm not afraid of Irontail," Peter told the Colonel confidently.

Peter Cottontail was so sure he was going to win, he threw a big victory party. He stayed up very late. Before he went to bed, Peter told his rooster alarm to wake him bright and early.

Irontail snuck into Peter's house and fed magic bubble gum to the rooster. The next morning, the rooster couldn't cock-a-doodle-doo! Peter slept on and on, all through Easter day.

No one wanted an egg from such a nasty bunny, so Irontail was only able to give away one.

But since Peter didn't deliver any eggs at all, Irontail won the contest!

Peter Cottontail knew he had let everybody down. He left April Valley, promising to make it up to them somehow.

After walking for days and days, Peter stumbled upon the Yestermorrow Mobile. It could transport anyone into yesterday or tomorrow.

Antoine the pilot agreed to take Peter back
to Easter so he could deliver his eggs—and win
the contest!

But not everything went as planned. Irontail discovered what Peter was up to and sent his spider to fiddle with the wires in the Yestermorrow Mobile.

Instead of traveling back in time
to Easter, Antoine and Peter flew
into a Fourth of July celebration.

"No one is going to want Easter eggs on the Fourth of July," Peter said sadly.

"Easter eggs, no. But Fourth of July eggs, maybe," suggested Antoine. "You just have to improvise."

Dressed as the Independence Day Bunny, Peter tried giving out red-white-and-blue eggs. But no one wanted them.

Next, Peter and Antoine flew into Halloween.
But no one wanted Peter's orange-and-black
eggs, either.

Peter then went to Christmas, but Irontail was
up to his old tricks again. He stole Peter's eggs!

Luckily, with the help of Santa Claus,
Peter got his eggs back.

The next stop was Valentine's Day. Peter painted
Valentine eggs. Surely someone would want them!

At a Valentine's Day party,
Peter gave a bunny named
Donna a red egg. She loved it!

Peter asked Donna to skate with him. Donna
put down her egg and they skated away.

When Peter wasn't looking, Irontail found the eggs and put an evil spell on them. The wicked bunny turned them green—inside and out!

Donna didn't want a green egg.

Luckily, Peter made a crash landing in Saint Patrick's Day.

Everywhere Peter looked, he saw green. Peter's green shamrock eggs soon became the hit of the Saint Patrick's Day parade. He gave them all away and finally won the contest!

Back in April Valley, Colonel Bunny congratulated Peter. "You have shown great ingenuity. Therefore, you have won the right to be the official Chief Easter Bunny," he said. Everyone cheered for Peter Cottontail!